Shadowville

Michael Bartalos

Viking

'Most every day
The sun shines bright
From six A.M.
Till six at night.

And where there's sun
And sky this blue
You're sure to see
A shadow too.

Shadow birds and shadow cats,

Shadow chefs in shadow hats.

Shadow
Farmers,
Shadow
Pigs,

Shadow
Barbers,
Shadow
Wigs.

They're busy till
The end of day,
Then quietly
They creep away.

'Cause in the night
There is no light,
And shadows
Disappear
From sight.

Shadow planes and shadow cars
Bring them all from near and far.

Crossing oceans and a hill,
They all head toward Shadowville.

Some will surf
And some will sail,
Some prefer
To come by whale.

Shadow
Cacti
From the Gobi
Stop for water in
Nairobi.

Then they walk
Without a stop
And never spill a single drop.

They've worked all day,
And now they're done,
It's time for them
To have some fun.

Shadows wearing
Shadow shorts
Spend the
Night at
Shadow sports.

They fold
And bend
And stretch like
Plastic.
While you sleep
They're quite
Gymnastic.

Shadow shoppers
And their friends
Shadow shop for
Fashion trends.

Everything from
Small to large,
Alterations
Free of charge.

Shadows order
All they want
At the shadow
Restaurant.

Though they've
Eaten
Huge amounts,
They still
Weigh only
Half an
Ounce.

According to the
Shadow map,
This is where
The shadows nap.

One short hour
In this tree
Restores their
Shadow energy.

When they wake they wash and scrub,
And shower in their shadow tub.

At five o'clock some shadows shave
Before they leave to start their day.

Shadow vans and shadow trains
Bring them back to us again.

Over oceans and a hill,
They say good-bye to Shadowville.

They take their places
One by one,
Underneath the
Morning sun.

'Cause where there's sun
And sky this blue,
You're sure to see
A shadow too.

For Georgia

VIKING
Published by the Penguin Group
Penguin Books USA Inc., 375 Hudson Street, New York, New York 10014, U.S.A.
Penguin Books Ltd, 27 Wrights Lane, London W8 5TZ, England
Penguin Books Australia Ltd, Ringwood, Victoria, Australia
Penguin Books Canada Ltd, 10 Alcorn Avenue, Toronto, Ontario, Canada M4V 3B2
Penguin Books (N.Z.) Ltd, 182–190 Wairau Road, Auckland 10, New Zealand

Penguin Books Ltd, Registered Offices: Harmondsworth, Middlesex, England

First published in 1995 by Viking, a division of Penguin Books USA Inc.

1 3 5 7 9 10 8 6 4 2

Copyright © Michael Bartalos, 1995
All rights reserved

LIBRARY OF CONGRESS CATALOGING-IN-PUBLICATION DATA
Bartalos, Michael.
Shadowville / Michael Bartalos.   p.   cm.
Summary: When night falls, shadows of all kinds flock to their private world where they play, eat, and rest.
ISBN 0-670-86161-8
[1. Shadows—Fiction. 2. Stories in rhyme.] I. Title.
PZ8.3.B25375Sh 1995 [E]—dc20 94-43070 CIP AC

Printed in USA
Set in Shadowville